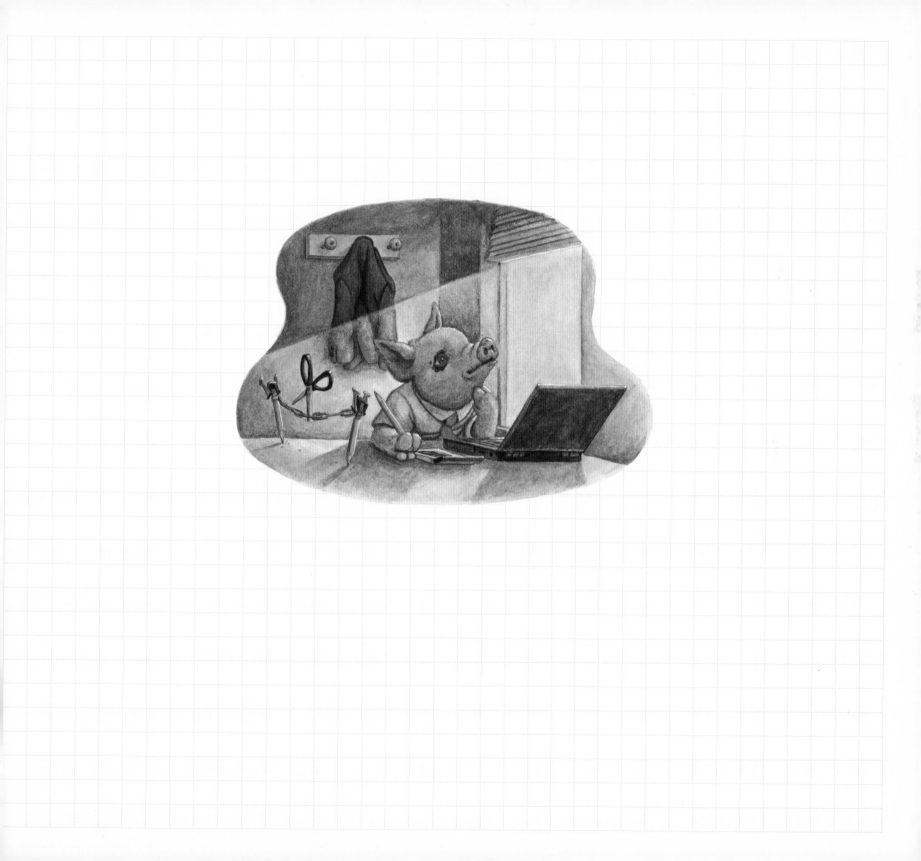

a good STory

Zack Rock

CREATIVE EDITIONS

Text and illustrations copyright © 2017 by Zack Rock Edited by Amy Novesky and Kate Riggs
Designed by Rita Marshall Published in 2017 by Creative Editions P.O. Box 227, Mankato, MN 56002 USA
Creative Editions is an imprint of The Creative Company www.thecreativecompany.us
All rights reserved. No part of the contents of this book may be reproduced by any means without the
written permission of the publisher. Printed in China Library of Congress Cataloging-in-Publication Data
Names: Rock, Zack, author, illustrator. Title: A good story / written and illustrated by Zack Rock. Summary:
In a world where numbers reign supreme, author and artist Zack Rock imagines a new story for Assistant
Bean Counter #1138, who dreams of an acrobatic life full of extraordinary possibility.
Identifiers: LCCN 2016056404 / ISBN 978-1-56846-280-6 Subjects: CYAC: 1. Self-realization—Fiction.
2. Counting—Fiction. 3. Numbers, Natural—Fiction. 4. Books and reading—Fiction.
BISAC: 1. JUVENILE FICTION/Business, Careers, Occupations. 2. JUVENILE FICTION/Science &
Technology. Classification: LCC PZ7.R5883 Goo 2017 / [E]—dc23 First edition 9 8 7 6 5 4 3 2 1

I never really felt like I fit **IN**.

Where I'm from, something only matters if it can be counted.

Assistant Bean Counter

that's me.

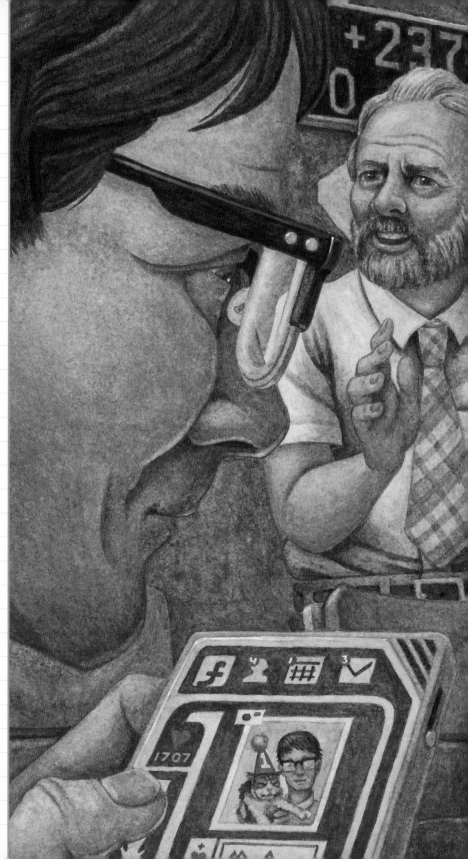

NUMBERS KEEP THE WORLD ORDERLY AND ORDINARY. YOU CAN ALWAYS COUNT ON NUMBERS!

At least, that's the story I grew up

.

2,276

6

20

9

63

0

432

10

367,449

31

8

We're supposed **TO** follow that old story without question, ignoring anything out of the ordinary. Even a change in the weather.

◄ But I'd rather not end up all wet.

I took cover in a strange store. Not a calculator in sight—just books!  in each one, a new story.

Pilots flew through fire. Kings had wings. Poets propped up the moon.

One called the sunset a glass of orange juice, spilled across the sky.

▼

I needed ese books!

(Also, I accidentally dropped a tower of books, showing off to the girl behind the counter. So I had to buy them.)

THe books contained possibilities beyond counting. AND among the candy-stripe tigers, whale islands, and Tyrannosaurus Texans, I found something really incredible: an acrobat.

Luckily one of **TH**ose books I dropped was a dictionary.

"Acrobat (/'akrəbat/) (noun): a performer who stands on his hands, flies with his feet, **AND** walks on wires."

That sounded awfully familiar.

But from **TH**e back of my mind, the old story still growled.

Anything out of the ordinary is dangerous, bean counter. There's safety in numbers!

Just **TH**en the girl from the bookstore entered. I casually caught her eye.

"You ever hear of an 'acrobat'?" I asked.

"Of course," she said, "Like you."

"Me? **NO**, I'm just a bean counter," I said.

"So?" she said. "**TH**at isn't you. Never let others write your story."

Suddenly, being more
than just a number

№ 1138

seemed as possible as an
ange juice sunset.

But  old story snarled at the idea.

You are Assistant Bean Counter #1138.
You are numbered. Your days are numbered.
You only count if you count.

Maybe that old story is right, **AND** I'm just another number to be ordered **AND** ordinary.

Now that's a good STory.